MW00791654

THE TINKER
OF
SALT COVE

BOOKS BY SUSAN HAND SHETTERLY

The Tinker of Salt Cove
The Dwarf Wizard of Uxmal
The New Year's Owl

THE TINKER

OF

SALT COVE

SUSAN HAND SHETTERLY

Illustrations By
SIRI BECKMAN

The Harpswell Press
Gardiner, Maine

Harpswell Press
The Boston Building
132 Water Street
Gardiner, Maine 04345

The Tinker of Salt Cove is partially funded by a grant from the
Maine Arts Commission.

Designed on Crummett Mountain by Edith Allard
Imagesetting by High Resoultion, Inc.
Camden, Maine
Printing and binding by Meriden-Stinehour Press
Lunenburg, Vermont

Library of Congress Catalog Card Number
90-80832

ISBN 0-88448-080-1

ACKNOWLEDGEMENTS

With special thanks to my husband, Robert, whose
patient help guided the first drafts of this book, and to
Carle Gray of Sullivan, Maine, whose careful reading
kept it honest.

This book is dedicated to my mother,
Dorothy Ryan Hand,
who felt most at home in small New England towns.

Author's Note

John Cling was a real person who disembarked from a salt ship at the town of Sullivan, Maine in the last years of the nineteenth century. He was a tinker. He traveled the coastal roads of Hancock and Washington Counties on poles, or stilts. He lived under a boat. Most of the details in this story correspond to what is recorded about him in Sullivan annals.

All other characters in this story are inventions of the author, except for Captain True who was, in fact, the captain of a steamer named the *Buttercup* and Wolf Lipsky, who was an itinerant salesman.

THE TINKER
OF
SALT COVE

ONE

Nothing blows as sharp as April wind. When it comes off the bay it smells of salt and of the deep, wintry ocean beyond.

In the town of Salt Cove, the hillside that looked down at the harbor docks and out across the bay was winter-bare in the early spring. No trees grew on it the way they do today. And the houses were few.

Lizzie Ashe and I trudged home alongside the wagon ruts of the road after school let out. Some evenings we raced across the hill until our mothers called us in through the early dark.

Lizzie's braids flared wet and stringy when she ran. Our dresses slapped against our legs, and the wind took our voices and blew them back at us like echoes. Above us, a few woodcocks, as brown as last year's leaves spun into the air making a twittering sound with their wings and, singing a lispy two-note, fell back to earth again.

"Elizabeth!" Lizzie's mother leaned out the kitchen door of her house, the white apron tied to her waist snapping brightly. "Supper!" she wailed.

Then my mother came to the shed door of our house. "Maude!" she cried.

Lizzie and I would pick up our books and brush off our skirts and walk home.

The April that I remember, the snow had melted. The harbor was free of ice and alive with quick, dark water. Mud glistened in the wagon ruts of the road.

A four-masted schooner out of Liverpool, the *Mary Ellen*, was the first ship in the spring to tie up at the harbor. She brought salt in sackcloth bags from England for the fishing fleets, and for people up and down this part of the coast to use to dry strip-fish.

Everyone thought her captain was a stalwart man. No matter the weather, the *Mary Ellen* always looked so jaunty, so ready to ride any wind. The men of Salt Cove would talk about the days of the great schooners, about the old captains they remembered and of the beautiful old ships. It was a shame, they said, that all this seemed to be coming to an end.

One evening Lizzie and I sat down on the hill to watch the *Mary Ellen*'s sailors row to the dock. Hiram Emery, the owner of the general store where the salt was sold, hurried along to meet them, waving his arms. Mr. Emery was a stocky man with a big gray beard.

"Look!" Lizzie poked me in the side. I turned to see the corner of a lace curtain lift at the second story bedroom window of a house across the way. It was Miss Simpson. Her dark gaze shot straight across the harbor to the ship. Lizzie and I put our heads in our skirts and laughed. We knew that Miss Simpson had an eye for the captain.

Ten minutes later, she closed the door of the house and walked to the road toward the docks. In her shiny black shoes she stepped lightly over the wagon ruts and the deepest puddles. We watched the wind whip at her black hat. The brim flapped around her face as if she were wearing a captive bird.

The sailors had gathered with Mr. Emery at the dock. Some of them were lighting pipes; Lizzie and I could smell the faint drift of English tobacco. We heard Mr. Emery's booming guffaw and saw how he threw back his head when he laughed. And when we saw that, we laughed too.

Then Lizzie and I noticed the young captain take a little step forward. He lifted his hat and bowed, ever so slightly, to Hattie Simpson. And she curtsied right back to him, right there in the middle of the muddy road.

At the far side of the big dock a gesture caught our attention. A stranger slipped in front of the old scrap barrel. He jumped down to the seaweed on the rocks where the tide had pulled away and hurried over it up the bank to the road.

Miss Simpson turned to watch him, too. He was very tall and thin. He moved in a graceful, secret way, like a fox does when it crosses an open field to the shelter of the woods.

Our eyes trailed him along the road. The sun was setting fiery red behind a line of black spruces. The man seemed to walk into the trees and the sunset and disappear.

"Who's that?" Lizzie whispered.

"I don't know ..." I answered. But suddenly I felt uneasy.

"Elizabeth!"

"Maude!"

The voices fell out of the wind. We stood up, our skirts soaked through, and walked home.

* * *

The first week in May, I planted peas in the kitchen garden that we kept out back, pushing the dry, wrinkled seeds fingerdeep into ground that felt as if it had just let go the last of its ice. By the time I'd covered them up and patted them in, it was nightfall.

Soaking my hands in a pan of soapy water at the sink, I was looking vaguely out the kitchen window when I saw a light. It was no bigger than a candle might make, flickering out by Mr. Emery's big old dory that lay above the beach beyond the docks. The dory had been hauled out and turned over years ago.

"Ma!" I called. Together we looked through the clean hushed darkness.

"It's Hiram," she decided. "Why, he must be out poking around that old wreck of his."

But I wasn't so sure. Mr. Emery didn't seem the sort to be looking for something down by the water after dark.

The next day, as Lizzie and I walked home from school, I said, "A candle was burning out by the old dory last night."

"Ma says it was Mr. Emery," I added. I could see that Lizzie was thinking it over.

"Let's go look," she said at last, and we turned past the Widow Hooper's place, into the field at the back of the store. The field rose to a small bluff before the bay, and on it Mr. Emery collected things that most people haul to their dumps in the woods. He kept cracked iron sinks and rusted plows without handles or blades. A carriage lay on its side, the left wheels gone. A gunnel with peeling red paint leaned on top of a schooner spar. Shaped like the face of a grinning cat, an iron door knocker, rusted and broken, leered up at us from the new grass.

The grass was very green. As we walked across it, stepping over Mr. Emery's things, the field rose gradually toward the bluff.

Laying our books aside, we crawled up to where we could look down at the old dory. I remember three herons standing in the shallows, the tide at dead low, and how the gray, smooth mud along the shore shone like polished pewter.

Across the hull of Mr. Emery's boat salt sacks were spread. I can close my eyes and see the black block printing on them still: SCHOFIELD'S SALT, LIVERPOOL, ENGLAND. The boat was propped up at the stern and a ring of stones beside it contained a cooking fire.

At the far side of the dory a man stood up. It was the same man we had watched walk into the sunset.

"You!" Lizzie cried. He startled and jumped back.

No more than a few seconds passed before we shot away, grabbed our books, and dashed for the road. But it seemed like an hour.

The man's face was very pale. He wore a salt sack for a shirt. I remember that his eyes, as they stared up at us, were deep blue, and his face was fine drawn. But there was something about him that set us back.

He wasn't like anyone Lizzie or I had ever seen before.

When we reached the road we were panting. "What was that?" I gasped.

"Our secret," Lizzie solemnly answered.

In a small town there are few secrets. So we decided that the man at Mr. Emery's dory would be ours. But no one could live in the town or walk out on the docks or along the road to the north without noticing before long the smoke, curling from his fire, that sometimes hung in the air above the little cove where the boat lay, or the candle that sometimes burned into the dark.

Two

In late spring the weather warmed and the days were long.

Mr. Emery unlocked the big oak door of his general store promptly at eight o'clock Mondays through Saturdays. We bought tea, sugar, tobacco, candles, coffee, sea biscuits, salt pork, hammers, flour, matches, saw blades, and, of course, salt from Mr. Emery. But his place was more than a store. Inside we learned the daily news of neighbors.

Lizzie and I would buy a paper cone full of lemon candies for a penny and sit out on the store porch, listening to the talk, the sudden laughter, and the bustle of the people inside. We smelled the scents that wafted through the open windows from the molasses and the salt pork barrels every time Mr. Emery lifted a lid. We'd sit in the sun alert to the voices at our backs and watch the people passing on the road.

But that wasn't the only way we kept up with the world. There were tinkers and peddlers too, people who walked into town carrying sacks filled with things to sell. They knocked at the side doors of our houses and when one of us, busy with chores, stepped out, they extolled the virtues of whatever it was they were carrying. Some, like Wolf Lipsky, arrived in a buggy. Mr. Lipsky had a black horse named Mouse who gently snuffled the palms of our hands searching for sugar. My mother and Lizzie's mother — and almost everyone else's mother — bought their house dresses from Mr. Lipsky. And sometimes one of our fathers would pick out a formal suit. He would step into the parlor room to put it on and come back outside again so that Mr. Lipsky could measure and tuck and turn our serious fathers slowly around by the shoulders as if they were boys again. Mr. Lipsky judged the fit, saying, "Just so," or "A *nip* there. Only a nip." Where he'd find the need for a nip, Mr. Lipsky would jab in a straight pin and instruct our mothers to sew along the seam, not altering what he called the *flow* of the suit.

A scissor grinder who spoke no English and always wore a black jacket and a white shirt with no collar and carried his whetstone in a leather strap across his back arrived every summer. Saying incomprehensible things, he would wave a child of the house off to fill his water pail. I remember pouring a thin, even ribbon of water out of the pail and onto the whirring whetstone. We watched him set the blades of our knives and scissors, one after another, precisely against the rim. The high grating shriek shivered in our ears, and a fine dust floated away. The man would look into our faces then and grin, showing his shiny gums with one dark tooth sticking up from the lower jaw.

Each spring, a tall Passamaquoddy woman with a stern face sold my mother a bottle of something she called *Sagwa*. My mother believed that it gave us strength; she took one spoonful each morning. So did my father and I. Sagwa tasted mysteriously cool, sweet, and spicy.

* * *

One afternoon, as Lizzie and I sat on the porch of Mr. Emery's store savoring our supply of lemon sours, Gavin Jakes, the captain of the *Mary Ellen*, accompanied Miss Simpson through the door.

"Well, Hiram," we heard him say as he stepped to the counter, "I see you've put my passenger up in a first-class hotel."

Mr. Emery laughed.

"He's a peculiar sort, that man," the captain continued. "I suppose I'll check my first mate's story on him once I get back to Liverpool. I've always accused Mr. Rooney of liking fiction more than he likes facts."

"And what might that fiction be?" inquired Mr. Emery softly.

"Well, sir," Hattie Simpson interjected, "it seems we've got a murderer on our hands!"

"I doubt it," the captain said. Lizzie and I heard the store suddenly quiet. Everyone inside must have turned to the captain and Hattie Simpson.

"I don't think he's a fugitive," the captain went on. "He was decent and polite on board. And he more than paid his way. In gold, as a matter of fact. He didn't know much about sailing, but he'd do whatever chore I bade him. A curious thing — he'd never give us a last name. 'What's your name?' we'd ask. 'John,' he'd say."

"Mostly he sat up on deck, looking out over the water. He's a sad one, I can tell you that, but not a murderer. And I consider myself a judge of character." From the window where Lizzie and I were watching now, we saw him look down and smile fondly at Miss Hattie Simpson, as if she somehow proved his point.

"Mr. Rooney says that he's an earl's son," she persisted, in a mock whisper. "And that he killed his own dear sweetheart, fleeing the bloody scene in the dark of midnight and wandering desolate over the countryside. Crazy with grief, Mr. Rooney says."

"Why did he do it?" old Flossey Colby's words rasped out of her throat.

"Jealousy!" Hattie Simpson triumphed. "He couldn't stand the thought of losing her."

As I held my breath and put my hand to my neck, I heard Lizzie bite down on her lemon sour.

"That Hattie," she said as she chewed, "is a real actress."

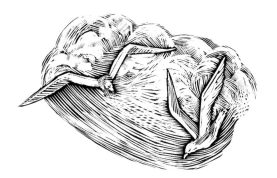

THREE

That spring the men of the town burned the blueberry fields. The line of their fire moved in the night across the unseen hills above the town like a red serpent slowly writhing in the sky. Afterward the air smelled acrid and the hills looked charred. But a rush of new, deep green sprang up. The only darkness we saw on the hills then, other than a few burned stumps, was an occasional black bear shuffling across the young berry plants.

Lizzie and I watched for smoke from the little ring of stones by the dory. When we saw it, whispy before the spruces of Little Salt Island, a shiver went through us. When we didn't see it, we worried too, about where the man might be, and what he might be doing.

We had heard people mention him only occasionally. Until ice-up our town was busy with boats pulling in and sailors from far away ports crowding our docks. The man that Lizzie and I had seen at the dory seemed to sink into the general rush and flurry of the summer. No one else had time to try to figure him out. Lizzie and I spoke of him; we went over and over the moment we saw him from the edge of the bluff.

* * *

My father was Amos True, captain of the *Buttercup*, the daily steamer that ran from Little Salt past Bean Island to Mount Desert and back. The *Buttercup* carried mail, salt, tombstones, and passengers. In summer my father might take a farmer's garden vegetables over to Mount Desert to sell, and sometimes he would return with rusticators. They were people from away who brought clothes in big wicker hampers and put up for a week or more at the Waukeag Hotel. Lizzie and I liked to stroll by every so often to see the city people in their country clothes. They sat out on the wide white veranda in rocking chairs, wrapped up against the air off the water, reading books as they rocked and slapping a few mosquitos that droned out of the damp woods around the town on late summer afternoons.

In the evenings my mother and I watched for the *Buttercup* out beyond Bean Island. When we saw her smokestack, we would put a pot of potatoes, or whatever else we had, to boil on the woodstove and set the table for supper. By the time my father reached the house, everything was ready.

"I had quite a passenger today," he chuckled one evening as he stuffed a corner of his napkin into the collar of his shirt.

"The man that lives under Hiram's dory came back over with me." I gasped. Lizzie and I had seen no smoke for weeks. We had decided that the fire on the hills must have scared him off.

"You'd never guess his line of work: he's a tinker," my father continued. "A tinsmith. And he mends clocks. Those old salt sacks of Hiram's he's made into a pair of pants and a shirt for himself. Nothing Wolf Lipsky would approve of, of course. But the oddest thing about him is that he walked to the *Buttercup* on stilts as if he were a circus clown ... I'd never seen anything like it."

"What a peculiar man!" my mother laughed.

Afterward, I lay in bed thinking. I knew what circuses and clowns were because I had read about them in books. I thought of the stilts and the salt sacks and that narrow, pale face that seemed so out of place among us.

The full moon rose in the sky. Ever so gradually, it moved higher and was cut by a window sash. Then it slid beyond the sash and shone at the center of a pane, its shape distorted by the waves and bubbles in the glass.

I tried to sleep but couldn't. Turning to study the moon again, I watched its light stream into the bristles of my hairbrush that lay on the dresser by the window. Then it moved to the small china dog my father had brought me from Mount Desert. It caught in the painted eyes so that the dog seemed to gaze at me, quietly, across the still air of my room.

Very gradually, the moonlight edged away across the dresser. I thought again of the man off the *Mary Ellen*.

By the first light of morning, I knew there was no point lying in bed anymore. I saw, as the dark drained away, that the harbor was lost in a bank of sea fog through which only two ship's masts and a gray winged gull showed — the gull flying out, then turning back and disappearing.

I dressed in a hurry. No one was moving in the town. No lights shown from any windows. It must have been a little before four o'clock because at that hour some neighbors and my father, too, would be lighting their lamps.

Drawing the shed door shut behind me, I stepped into the damp cold and moved toward the sound of water: the easy, even lapping on the rocks along the shore, and the drumming against an unseen hull.

Sea fog changes a place. Shapes of familiar things such as trees or houses suddenly stand before you as if they had moved on their own.

I reached the road. The fog parted. Where it had been, something tall and dark now stood. It was the tinker.

Balanced on the stilts, he was almost eight feet tall. His bare feet splayed on the wooden wedges. His arms were wrapped around the poles. For what seemed a long time, we stared at each other.

I opened my mouth to cry out. But, all at once, he vanished. Only the fog rose up in front of me.

FOUR

"He's got to go, Hiram!" It was Oscar Chilcott speaking.

"Now, Oscar, don't get your dander up — what do you have against the man?"

Ma had asked me to run down to the store for a bag of white flour. It was five minutes to closing time. Four men stood at the counter across from Mr. Emery.

No one had seen me slip in through the open doorway. I stood against the salt pork barrel and waited.

"We've got someone living under a stove-up boat — a stanger who wears unsightly clothes and hardly talks to anyone! He's peculiar, Hiram. And some people in the town consider him a danger." George Dunbar pressed the palms of his hands into the counter and leaned toward Mr. Emery.

"You don't want someone killed here. You don't want to be the cause of that!" Mr. Emery didn't flinch.

"Who's talking of killing, George?" he said. "It seems to me we're getting ahead of ourselves.

"You can't run someone out of a town because of the way he dresses or because you don't like where he lives. You've let all manner of peddlers and tinkers sell you goods up to your place at one time or another, George. This man — odd as he is — has an honest trade. He works. And there are some you can't say that about." Mr. Emery glanced sideways at Henry Bean. I watched Mr. Bean draw back and stare down at the floor.

"When you can fix a clock or mend a pot better than the man who sleeps under my dory — and pays me rent for it — then, George, I'll allow you to march over my field and run him out."

Mr. Emery turned his back to them and began stacking cakes of laundry soap on a shelf. The men left, and I stepped up to the counter.

"Mr. Emery?" I asked. He startled and turned.

"Well, hello, Maude. It's awful late for a lemon sour."

"Ma wants a bag of white flour. Mr. Emery?"

"Yes?"

"About that man…"

"The tinker?" Mr. Emery sighed and looked at me thoughtfully. "You're not afraid of him too, are you, Maude?" he asked.

"I don't know who he is…," I began.

"You don't know who he was, Maude. He is pretty much what you see. A queer sort, to be sure." Mr. Emery let his eyes wander over the room. The tin lantern that hung from the ceiling bathed everything in its soft, yellow half-light.

"You've got the world ahead," he continued. "But I doubt you'll ever come upon anyone quite like him again. And one's probably enough — at least for a small town," he smiled.

"Was he an earl's son?" I blurted. Mr. Emery laughed.

"Maybe he was. Now he's just a poor tinker under a

[24]

very drafty dory.   He sort of washed up here, didn't he, Maude? Like an old spar broken off a ship that's gone down."

F~IVE~

It wasn't until the next spring, after the tinker had spent the winter under the dory that Captain Jakes sailed back to Salt Cove on the *Mary Ellen* and let it be known at Mr. Emery's store that he had heard no mention at all along the docks of Liverpool about a fugitive. You could tell Miss Simpson was disappointed.

"Humph!" she snorted. "Just goes to show he was born rich and his family hushed up the whole sorry story ." Lizzie laughed when Hattie Simpson said that. And then she blushed when the woman turned sharply and stared her down.

Along the coastal towns, from Salt Cove to Eastport, there was talk. The railroad line was being laid down out of Bangor. You could almost feel it coming through the soles of your shoes, a trembling in the ground that meant new things.

Mr. Emery said that the railroad would end the days of peddlers and tinkers. There'd be no need for them when the trains from the cities brought goods to the people in the towns, he explained.

The tinker could make Machias from Salt Cove — more than fifty miles on the coast road — before sunset in summer. His stilts gave him a five-foot stride, and at full speed he looked more like a loon slapping across the bay before it throws itself into the air. When he came to a farmer's stone wall, he braced the stilts on the near side, took a leap, and vaulted over the stones with room to spare.

Away from the dory, it was said that he slept in fields, or on the banks of streams. I watched him carefully when he came into town. And I knew he knew I watched him. But we didn't speak.

He wore cooking pots tied to a rope across his shoulders. If the wind was right, you could hear them before he crossed the west ridge. As he loped along on his stilts, some children rushed from their houses and chased after him in the dust of the summer road crying, "John! John! The cling-clang man!" And most townspeople called him John Cling as if a part of the noise that trailed him were his legitimate name.

Nobody could make out how he maneuvered those stilts or why he wouldn't rather keep a horse, like Wolf Lipsky. A few pairs of stilts appeared — almost self-consciously — in Salt Cove and were tried out in back fields. My father whittled braces to fit the arches of my feet and attached them to poles. I got so I could walk turns around the house on them. But John Cling ran. Or galloped. It was as if they were extensions of his own legs and not something he had to think about, as other people did.

* * *

After school ended for the summer, Lizzie and I didn't have much time to spend together. Her father was working on a fishing boat and wouldn't be back until the fall. Lizzie's mother put her in charge of her baby sister, the milk cow, and the chickens. My chores were over by mid-day. In the afternoons I walked around town or read books or played with other friends. But I missed Lizzie.

An afternoon in August when the water glinted so brightly out in the harbor that it was painful to look at, I saw Miss Nellie Havey walk sharply to the old elm in her front yard carrying a tall pitcher and a glass on a tray. The tinker sat with his back against the elm, leaning forward, the pieces of one of Miss Havey's Chinese parlor clocks spread out before him in the grass. I supposed Miss Havey was carrying switchel because that was what most people drank on summer days. It was made out of the coldest well water mixed with white sugar and vinegar. Nothing tastes quite so good as a glass of switchel.

Miss Havey's housedress blew around her thin knees as she walked. I watched as she bent down, ever so carefully, to hand the tinker the glass.

Her father, Captain Josiah Havey, had been one of Salt Cove's most important citizens. For twenty years he was master of big and famous barks that sailed to South America and across the Pacific Ocean. He took his wife and their daughter Nellie on board. They brought back big painted urns from China. And trinkets of carved scrim-shaw. They brought trunks made out of sandalwood that smelled like hot, flowery jungles when you opened them. And they brought back wool rugs. When Mrs. Havey died in Singapore, Nellie was five years old. The Captain sent his daughter back here to her Aunt Amanda who raised her in the house by the docks, full of all those beautiful faraway things.

At the school, Ma said that Nellie Havey's eyes always seemed to be looking into a great distance. "Ocean eyes," Ma called them.

When the Captain retired, Miss Nellie cared for him in the big house. That's when Ma would dress me up and take me over for a visit some Saturday afternoons. After the Captain died, Miss Nellie hardly stepped outside again, and she didn't have company on Saturday afternoons anymore. We saw her at church, or hurrying along the road to Mr. Emery's store. But she never stopped to chat with neighbors.

I noticed, as a little girl, how small her hands were. Fine boned, like the rest of her. She seemed more a queer bird than a person. And her voice had a high chirpy sound when she spoke. But when she sang in church, it seemed a thing apart. It was lovely to hear, like the voice of a hermit thrush calling just before dark from the deep quiet of the woods: that lifting, bell-like, solitary sound.

As I slowly walked by Miss Havey's house that long and radiant summer afternoon, I saw her smile down at John Cling. I hadn't seen her smile in years.

* * *

One day the same summer, my father took me to Mount Desert on the *Buttercup* and we walked the streets past the fine houses behind their picket fences. When we tied up at the dock at Salt Cove it was still light, and we could see from the water that the tinker sat on our front lawn, with the clock that had belonged to my mother's grandmother. I hoped that he wouldn't finish with it before I'd helped my father at the steamer. "Go on up," my father said.

So, I walked up the hill and sat down on the grass next to the tinker. His long, sensitive fingers extracted the gears and the metal ribbons and the little weights from the body of the clock, and lay them, precisely, in the grass. He didn't seem to mind my watching, although he didn't talk. He sat on a barrel top that he had brought along as if it were a little stool.

Above us, cliff swallows twittered as they flew back and forth to the eaves of the house. As the day slowly turned into evening, and the swallows took one more swoop around the hill and dipped into their nests, my mother brought out a tray with bowls of potato salad and peas and a plate of biscuits. My father followed with a pitcher of switchel. I hurried into the kitchen and grabbed plates and forks. It was dusk as we ate, sitting in a semicircle, facing the water.

My parents chatted together as the old clock ticked steadily. It was peaceful, somehow, even though the tinker said no more than, "Thank you," or "I'd like another biscuit, if you please," in a brisk accent that was new to me. We didn't mind his silence because it seemed friendly. And even though I tried not to watch him eat, I noticed that every gesture he made was precise and elegant.

After the tinker left, I saw Lizzie carrying her little sister across the lawn. She and I had promised to sneak out of our houses one night and meet on the hill when the moon shone directly above the bay.

"Tonight!" I yelled. She didn't hear me at first.

"What?"

"You know! Tonight!"

It was so late when at last I saw her running toward me in her white nightgown that I had almost given up waiting. We picked Queen Anne's lace and ox-eyed daisies and braided the stems into garlands by moonlight. We set the garlands on our heads. Silently, slowly, we danced down the hill to the big dock and sat with our feet over the edge, our toes trailing in the cold high tide.

The wide and barely stirring darkness seemed to lift us away from everything that was ordinary. For a long time, we sat on the dock hardly saying a word.

Then we saw the light. It shone from the parlor window of Miss Havey's house. You could notice it only if you were here, by the water, or farther up into the cove.

SIX

A year passed. Lizzie and I, and the rest of the people of the town it seemed, were growing used to the tinker. He was almost becoming a part of us. As strange as he was, he had chosen to live in our town and he helped to distinguish it from the other small towns along the coast.

The coast road carried news quickly. It moved like water in a river from one town down to the next.

That summer a story about the tinker poured into Salt Cove and it wasn't long before Lizzie and I knew it.

Racing on his stilts, John Cling had reached the outlying farms of Harrington around nightfall in a rainstorm. A local farmer, a Cowperthwaite, had offered him a bed. But the tinker asked to sleep in the barn — for he would never use a bed or even enter a house. When Mr. Cowperthwaite agreed, Cling announced that the rooster must be covered, so as not to crow.

The farmer didn't understand at first. He squinted, peering harshly at the tall pale man in wet salt sacks, holding his stilts in one hand as the rain streamed down his hair and pattered against the pots on his back. For some reason he could not fathom, the farmer saw that the tinker was afraid. So he turned toward the door of his house and called to one of his sons. He told him to set the rooster under a potato barrel. The son laughed. But when he saw the tinker, he hurried through the downpour to the barn and did as his father told him.

It was a steeply pitched barn, used to store salt hay cut on the Harrington marshes. Through it the rooster and a flock of hens wandered idly during the day. That night the hens perched on a stall door. John Cling lay down on the bare floor not far from them and not far from the rooster crouched in the pitch black under the barrel.

Mr. Cowperthwaite turned from the barn and left the tinker alone. The sky cleared during the night. A full moon rose.

At three thirty in the morning the farmer and his wife were jolted awake by a ghastly scream. They stumbled downstairs, flung the kitchen door wide, and rushed to the barn. The tinker had disappeared. A patch of silver light fell from the high window to an outline in the shape of a man that lay in the settled dust of the floor. And in the center of the moonlight stood the rooster, his legs wide, his little eyes burning. He lifted his head, flapped his wings, and crowed.

One of the farmer's sons had tipped up the barrel as a joke. "The sound that came wailing out of that madman," the farmer shuddered, "will haunt me forever."

"What's scary about a rooster?" Lizzie puzzled. I couldn't answer.

All week I had thought about the tinker. No one had seen him on the road. No one had seen him in another town fixing a clock or mending a housewife's broken pot.

I imagined him crouched somewhere, in the woods, perhaps, or along the rocks by the open bay. It made me sad to think of him so alone.

Seven

"I suppose you girls have heard about that tinker up to the Cowperthwaite's?" Miss Simpson stopped us in the road one windy afternoon when Captain Jakes was off to Boston and ports farther south.

"Yes, Ma'm," we answered. She stood with the autumn wind at her back. I noticed that she was pretty, her skin smooth and her eyes very shiny and dark. I hadn't thought about whether or not she was pretty before.

"Well!" she sniffed. I saw how fine and straight her features were and how she had pinned her black hair up high on her head, showing off her little white ears.

"Just goes to show!" she sniffed again.

I felt Lizzie stiffen next to me. She didn't want to ask Miss Simpson what she meant by "just goes to show." So I did.

"How is that Miss Simpson?"

"It's obvious, child! He was to be executed at dawn in some dreary English town — pulled from some damp and gloomy prison cell, shackled and in rags. The rooster's voice reminds him of the hour he escaped his just fate!" She watched the effect of her words as we stared at her, waiting eagerly for her to finish. But instead she laughed lightly, put a hand up to catch a curl that had fallen over her forehead, and continued down the road.

Lizzie shrugged.

"Let's have a look under the dory now that he's gone," I said.

The little cove where the dory lay was still, except for the sound of a stream nearby that splashed over the rocks in its hurry to the bay. A kildeer cried along the edge of the tide.

The dory had been recaulked with pine pitch. We ran our hands over the smooth, tight hull. Then we ducked down.

"Oh, how lovely!" Lizzie clapped her hands.

"Do you think he'll come back all of a sudden?" I asked, looking up toward the stream and the woods beyond.

"We won't stay long," Lizzie said. And she went in.

There was a table at the bow made out of a barrel top; its legs were three round stones. Toward the dory's stern a pallet was built and spread with neatly folded salt sacks. Shelves ran the length of the gunnels down to the ground. In them were plain necessities such as cooking pots, wooden spoons, candles, matches, a clam hoe, a jar of nails, and a book.

The dirt under the dory had been cobbled with flat stones. And right beyond the stern, a little stove leaned its black metal pipe out into the air.

"It's a playhouse!" exclaimed Lizzie. She crawled in and lay down on the pile of salt sacks. I reached for the book. *John Keats,* it said. The pages were waterstained and thin, almost translucent. It fell open, and I read:

O what can ail thee, knight-at-arms,
Alone and palely loitering?
The sedge has wither'd from the lake,
And no birds sing.

"Listen!" I called to Lizzie and read on:

O what can ail thee, knight-at-arms!
So haggard, and so woe-begone?
The squirrel's granary is full,
And the harvest's done.

I see a lily on thy brow
With anguish moist and fever dew,
And on thy cheeks a fading rose
Fast withereth too.

But she didn't listen.

"There's something under this sack," she said and yanked the pile aside. A small, bright object rattled to the stones. Lizzie picked it up. It was a locket ring with a tiny latch. When she opened it, we found two silhouettes, each covered by a piece of glass and framed with gold. They were two heads in profile. One belonged to a woman.

"Who do you think that is?" asked Lizzie. She pointed to the man.

"It's John Cling!" I said, amazed.

They were so little and so perfect. For a long time we stared at the stately profile of the woman.

It was almost night when we crawled out from under the dory. The long shadow of a spruce on the hill leaned across the hull.

I looked up and reached for Lizzie's arm. Straight ahead of us, against the parlor window of Miss Havey's house, shone that lonely light again.

"Maude," Lizzie said, "there are lots of lights on in the town this time of evening."

"But this one is different," I said.

Eight

Miss Hanna, our school teacher, allowed me to stay after, helping her wash the blackboards and sweep the floor and set logs in the woodbox for the next morning fire.

Out the big front window, I watched Lizzie walking home through the slanting copper light of late September. Nathaniel Preble often waited for her by the big white pine. He would take the books out of her arms, and they would turn away together down the path to the road.

Once, as Lizzie and Nathaniel disappeared around the bend in the path, I turned back to the school room, to its paper cutouts that decorated the walls and its shelves of worn books, and asked Miss Hanna, "Have you ever heard of John Keats?"

With a flourish she drew out a leather volume from the drawer of her desk and selected the poem that I had seen at the dory, "La Belle Dame Sans Merci."

"It is," she said, lowering her voice to a hush, "about a woman with no mercy … you shall see …"

> I saw pale kings and princes too,
> Pale warriors, death-pale were they all;
> They cried —'La Belle Dame sans Merci
> Hath thee in thrall!'

I saw their starved lips in the gloam,
With horrid warning gaped wide,
And I awoke and found me here,
On the cold hill's side.

After she stopped reading, I told Miss Hanna that I thought it was beautiful and frightening. She agreed. Then she turned a few pages crisply and began reading me a poem about a nightingale.

But I hardly listened. At last I thought I understood: the silhouette in the ring, the one with the slender neck and the high cheekbones, belonged to a woman John Cling had loved. A woman who had been cruel to him. Somehow I was sure of it. I thought of him, so far away from home, bent under that dory; and in its shadow reading and re-reading that poem.

John Cling had never killed anyone.

The light fell away from the window and a rush of wind spun the leaves of the maple tree by the door as Miss Hanna's calm, full voice read on.

It was almost dark when we locked the school door behind us and said goodnight at the bend in the path. As I walked home through the dusk, watching the waves rumple and white-cap in the outer harbor, I wondered again why no one had seen the tinker for a long time. Some people said he must have died. Others decided that he had returned to England on one of the schooners out of Bangor. I knew Miss Havey believed that the tinker was still alive, still here. Somewhere.

* * *

The last service on the lawn of the Church of Our Father was held on the first Sunday in October. All summer long — if the Sundays were fair — we would stand on the grass outside, our singing mixing with the keening sounds of ospreys and the grating calls of swallows.

That morning the October light lay hushed and almost hazy out over the unmoving bay. People stood on the grass in their Sunday best. My mother wore her navy blue with a high lace collar into which she had pinned her own mother's brooch. I wore my best brown serge. The fields around the town bloomed with the last flowers of the season, the blue asters and the thick spires of yellow goldenrod.

I stood between my parents half listening to Reverend Barnard's prayers. At the last hymn, "O God, Our Help in Ages Past," Miss Havey's voice seemed to shoot up like an arrow, trembling and sharp and true to each note.

All at once her voice was joined by another. I turned around. There stood the tinker.

With something almost like fear I turned back and listened to the tinker sing so heart-full and so clear. It seemed as if, for a moment, all of us on that hill became voices only, hovering above ourselves.

Before the service ended, the tinker leapt to his stilts and strode down the hill to the docks and hopped away between the seaweed-laden rocks. Beside him rushed a little dog.

Another year passed. The tinker came and went in an almost carefree spirit. I began to think that I had dreamed the time in the fog when he had looked so lost and ghostlike.

NINE

On the way to the school house in the early mornings, Lizzie and I would meet John Cling clattering along the road, his bright shining pots hanging from his shoulders. We would kneel down and gather up his little dog who loved to be scratched. Although he never spoke to us directly, sometimes, as he watched us with the dog, we heard him laugh. It was a soft, shy laugh and we kept our eyes averted for fear of somehow embarrassing him.

"I wonder what he calls his dog?" Lizzie said one day.

"I doubt he really talks to her," I said. "She just knows what he wants by watching him, I think."

"Well, what would you name her if she were yours?" Lizzie asked.

"I don't know. Maybe 'Agnes.'"

As fall drew on, and the weather cooled, the tinker began to change again. He looked restless and troubled. He kept himself more and more apart.

"I don't know how that fellow stays alive," Mr. Emery told my father. "Whatever food he buys — and it isn't much — I think he feeds to that dog of his."

"He seemed to be doing pretty well for awhile," my father said.

"I've even tried taking a pot of chowder and some

pork and cabbage down a few times. All he does is shake his head at me," Mr. Emery sighed.

His eyes drifted toward one of the store windows and my gaze followed his.

I had noticed that the tinker had not been stopping at Miss Havey's or at anyone else's house in town. If he was still mending and selling pots and fixing clocks, it was for strangers. I had passed Miss Havey's house and had seen her weeding her flower beds under the front windows, her gestures quick and peevish, as if her mind weren't on the task.

Outside the store, the dry October air raised miniature whirlwinds of dust along the road. Wolf Lipsky's horse, Mouse, stood at the tie-up, his muzzle deep in a feed bag. A farmer from Gouldsboro had just tied his horse next to Mouse and I watched as it turned and nosed at the bag.

Suddenly the horses shied. They jerked against their reins. A horrible scream ripped the air. I saw John Cling running up the road, his salt sack shirt hanging at his waist, his arms raised and trembling as if he had been struck by lightning.

Mr. Emery was out the door before I could speak, my father close behind him. I skirted the pork barrel and caught up with my father. But Mr. Emery didn't stop.

Neighbors stood aside as the tinker bolted up the road. Mr. Emery tore his apron off and ran after him. It hadn't occured to me that Mr. Emery knew how to run, but there he was in front of all of us reaching out, falling, and catching the tinker around the ankles, tripping him. The tinker dropped sideways. The little dog ran on in a streak of terror. Then she stopped, spun around, and dashed back to her master. John Cling just closed his eyes.

We watched Mr. Emery stand and dust off the front of his shirt. No one else moved except Miss Simpson, who clapped her hands together twice. Mr. Emery leaned down, scooped the tinker up and, holding him against his chest, carried him back down the road and into the store. The dog slipped in beside him just before he closed the door.

My father took my hand. "Let's go home," he said.

After supper my father put on his coat and hat, left the house, and walked down the hill to Mr. Emery's. He was gone a long time. When he came back his voice was heavy and tired.

"What gets into that tinker?" he said. "First a rooster. And then, out of nowhere, this! Hiram takes it pretty hard."

The woman in the ring rose up in front of my eyes.

"Maybe his heart is broken," I offered.

"I don't know about the man's heart," my father answered roughly, "but he refused to stay inside. He's back under the dory."

When I told Lizzie how the tinker had crumpled and fallen and how Mr. Emery had been so careful with him, tears welled up in her eyes.

"Let's take him something," she said. So we baked a pan of molasses cookies at her house and picked a nosegay of asters on the hill. As we crossed the field and drew close to the dory, we saw that a large tin was sitting at the bluff-edge.

"Whose is that?" demanded Lizzie.

"It's one of Miss Havey's old Chinese tea cannisters!" I exclaimed. It was painted with big green leaves and delicate white flowers. A painted yellow butterfly sat on one of the flower petals. Lizzie knelt down and pried the top off.

"Molasses cookies," she groaned. And I laughed. We set our cookies and the flowers next to the tin.

When we brought the tinker some shortbread the following week the cookies and the flowers were gone. A thread of smoke issued from the stove pipe at the boat. We peered down the bluff and saw the dog asleep on a salt sack.

"Maybe the dog ate the cookies," I whispered. Lizzie was busy prying off the lid of the cannister. Inside she found cubes of cheese and a handful of crackers wrapped in a pink napkin. Another napkin was tied around a pear. We laid the shortbread down and, quietly, we left.

* * *

Before the hard frost set, a work crew for the Shoreline Railroad dug along the banks on the other side of the bay. In the red earth close to the water, the men uncovered arrowheads and spear points and carved chunks of milky-colored quartz. The foreman dropped by the school with a box full of them for Miss Hanna. When I held those pieces of chipped and carved stone, a peculiar feeling came over me, even though I had known for some time that the town had not always been plain white houses and wide docks.

On Christmas Eve, when sea smoke hung in thick swirls above the black water and the afternoon sky faded to pale, shining pink, Lizzie and I set two warm loaves of anadama bread in the snow crust next to the intrepid tin. A package tied up in blue yarn lay in the snow as well. A note was attached to it: "Socks," it read, "from Mrs. Henry Bean."

Great thick plates of ice set over the bay in January. They heaved up on a high tide and crumbled and fell and froze together in a chaos of sharp angles. John Cling was the only tinker out on the road. He wore boots made of twine and salt sacks. In the deep snow, he lifted his little dog and carried her in a sack on his back. But he didn't stop to let us play with her anymore.

Hurrying on his stilts, he had time for no one. He looked as narrow and brittle as an icicle.

Miss Havey, sunk in a black coat that hung to her feet, and pulling an old grey shawl tight to her head, would smile wanly at us and say, "How do you do?" when Lizzie and I met her along the road.

"She knows we know about her Chinese tin," Lizzie said.

T EN

After I had finished studying, while my parents slept, I would sometimes throw on my father's greatcoat and pull up my boots and walk down to the bay just to see if Miss Havey had set her lantern in the window.

I would stand by the docks and stare at the light. I found its steady yellow flame welcoming, although I knew that it was not for me.

One steel-cold February dawn a persistent cry woke me. A dog was howling — a long, drawn out sound like the wail a wolf might make.

"Father!" I yelled. We dressed in the grey light. Neighbors, one after another, joined us as we sprinted and slipped along the shore to the cove. Lizzie ran next to me and squeezed my hand as we hurried.

It was John Cling's dog howling at the side of the dory. My father leaned under the boat.

"He's dead," I heard him say. "Frozen."

The sun was beginning to rise across the bay when Lizzie's father, Mr. Emery, and my father crawled under and drew the body out. We watched them set John Cling on a wooden pallet. He was straight and terribly thin, with his arms neatly folded over his chest.

Above the dory on the bluff someone who had come

running had kicked over Miss Havey's tin. It lay open and empty on its side in the broken snow.

The men lifted the body into the blazing early light and carried it up the hill. "Oh, Lizzie, look!" I cried. On the tinker's right hand the sun caught and briefly held the glitter of his ring.

* * *

"Miss Havey!" Lizzie called as she let fall the brass knocker. After a long wait we heard slippers shuffling across a bare wood floor. Nellie Havey opened the door just a crack, her eyes so wide and bruised looking that we knew she had seen it all.

"We thought you'd like to have his dog," I said holding out the trembling animal that I had carried from the dory. She didn't seem to understand. So I said it again. And then she looked down at the cold creature as if she had known it somewhere before.

"No," she said. And the door closed.

My mother made me wash the dog three times in the tin tub we used for ourselves on Saturdays. I heated water on the cookstove and scrubbed and rinsed and scrubbed again. Slowly the dust of the road and the terrible cold of the dory seemed to drain away from the little dog. She lay, quietly, curled up under the woodstove, her soft fur drying to a dark gold.

At nightfall, I picked her up and carried her to my bed.

She slept at the foot. When I woke, once, to make sure she was still there, the moonlight shone gently on her and on the china dog, whose eyes, once again, seemed filled with a light of their own.

The next night I left the house and walked with the dog to the bay. There was no moon. The black hill dropped to the black water. And from the parlor window of Miss Havey's house, no light shone.